HANSEL AND DIESEL

Written and illustrated by

DAVID GORDON

LAURA GERINGER BOOKS
An Imprint of HarperCollins*Publishers*

Hansel and Diesel

Copyright © 2006 by David Gordon   Manufactured in China.

Library of Congress Cataloging-in-Publication Data
Gordon, David, date
    Hansel and Diesel / written and illustrated by David Gordon.— 1st ed.
        p.   cm.
    "Laura Geringer Books."
    Summary: Sibling trucks Hansel and Diesel travel into the middle of the junkyard in
search of fuel and have a frightening encounter with the Wicked Winch.
    ISBN-10: 0-06-058122-0 (trade bdg.) — ISBN-10: 0-06-058123-9 (lib. bdg.)
    ISBN-13: 978-0-06-058122-0 (trade bdg.) — ISBN-13: 978-0-06-058123-7 (lib. bdg.)
    [1. Trucks—Fiction. 2. Winches—Fiction. 3. Automobile graveyards—Fiction. 4. Brothers
and sisters—Fiction.] I. Title.
PZ7.G6547Han 2006
[E]—dc22   2005013911
                                                                                    CIP
                                                                                    AC

Typography by Neil Swaab
1 2 3 4 5 6 7 8 9 10
❖
First Edition

For Dad and Marcia Gordon

At the edge of a huge junkyard lived brother and sister pickup trucks. Their names were Hansel and Diesel.

Hansel and Diesel were hungry. Fuel was getting low.
"We're running out of gas," said their father.
"I don't know how we'll make it through the winter," their mother agreed.

Hansel and Diesel were listening from their room.
"I think we should go out to look for some fuel," said Diesel.

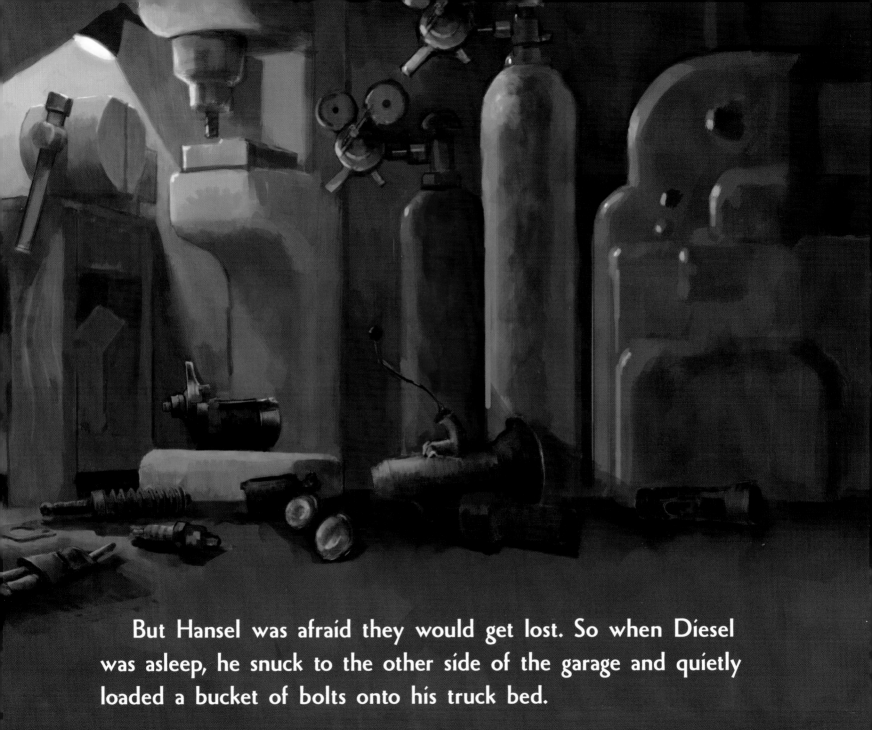

But Hansel was afraid they would get lost. So when Diesel was asleep, he snuck to the other side of the garage and quietly loaded a bucket of bolts onto his truck bed.

Early the next morning, while the sun was rising, Hansel and Diesel left home. As they traveled deeper and deeper into the junkyard, Diesel noticed that Hansel was going very slowly and went out of his way to hit every bump on the path.

"What are you doing, Hansel?" she said. "You'll ruin your wheels that way!"

"I'm leaving a trail of bolts so we know our way home," said Hansel, jiggling more bolts loose from his bucket.

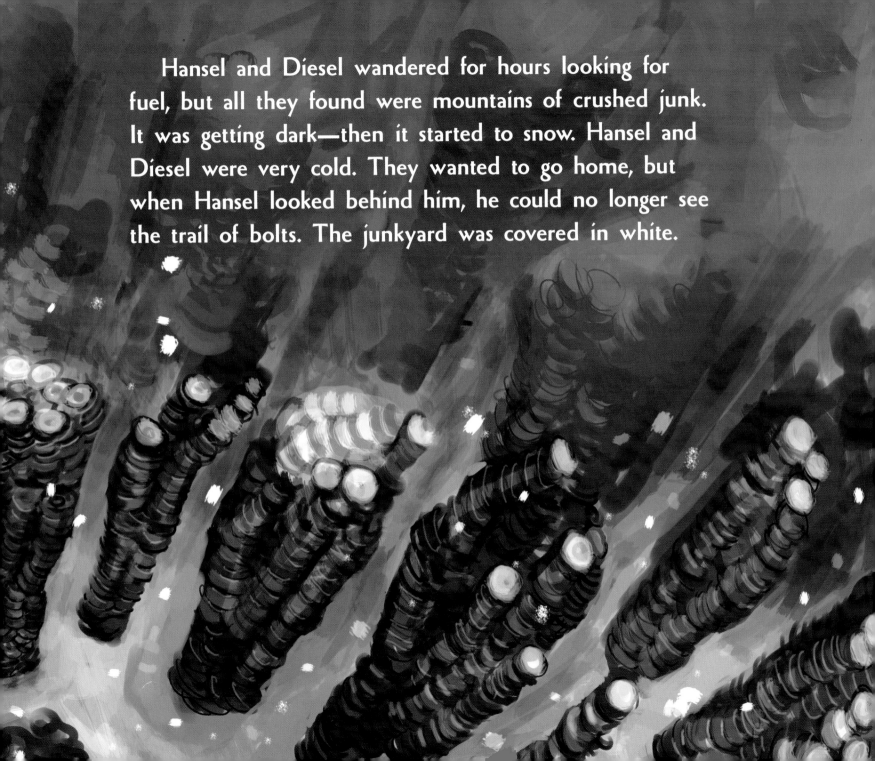

Hansel and Diesel wandered for hours looking for fuel, but all they found were mountains of crushed junk. It was getting dark—then it started to snow. Hansel and Diesel were very cold. They wanted to go home, but when Hansel looked behind him, he could no longer see the trail of bolts. The junkyard was covered in white.

Hansel thought he saw a flash of light in the darkness. The trucks plodded ahead, and as they got closer, they saw brightly colored lights, shiny gas pumps, huge tanks full of fuel, and piles and piles of brand-new tires. It was the most beautiful gas station they could have imagined, and it was right in the middle of the junkyard!

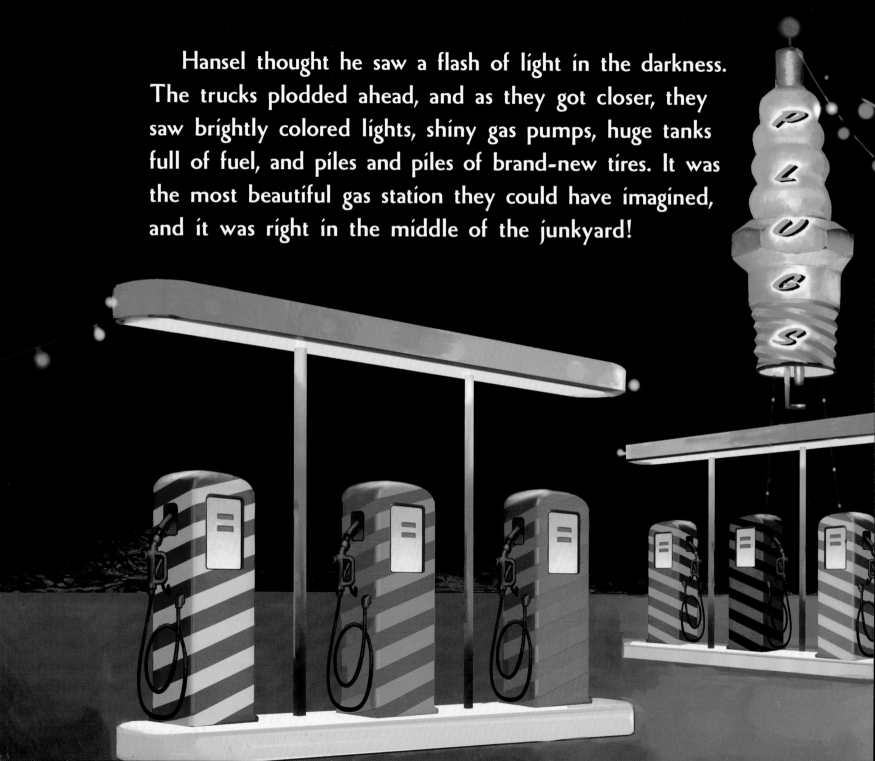

Hansel and Diesel were cold and very hungry.
They drank deeply from the warm fuel tanks.
Then they heard a voice say, "Guzzle, guzzle,
drip and drool, who is drinking all my fuel?"

And a little old winch came out from inside
the gas station.
"Poor little trucks," she said. "There's plenty
more. Why don't you follow me into the garage?"

The winch placed two small barrels of warm oil in front of them.
"My little darlings," she said when they had finished, "you must
be tired. Why don't you back up and sleep on my lifts?"
And Hansel and Diesel fell into a deep sleep.

In the middle of the night, Hansel and Diesel were awakened by a horrible noise. The garage door was closing! Huge, screaming saw blades appeared on the floor and on the ceiling. Hansel and Diesel were going to be shredded!

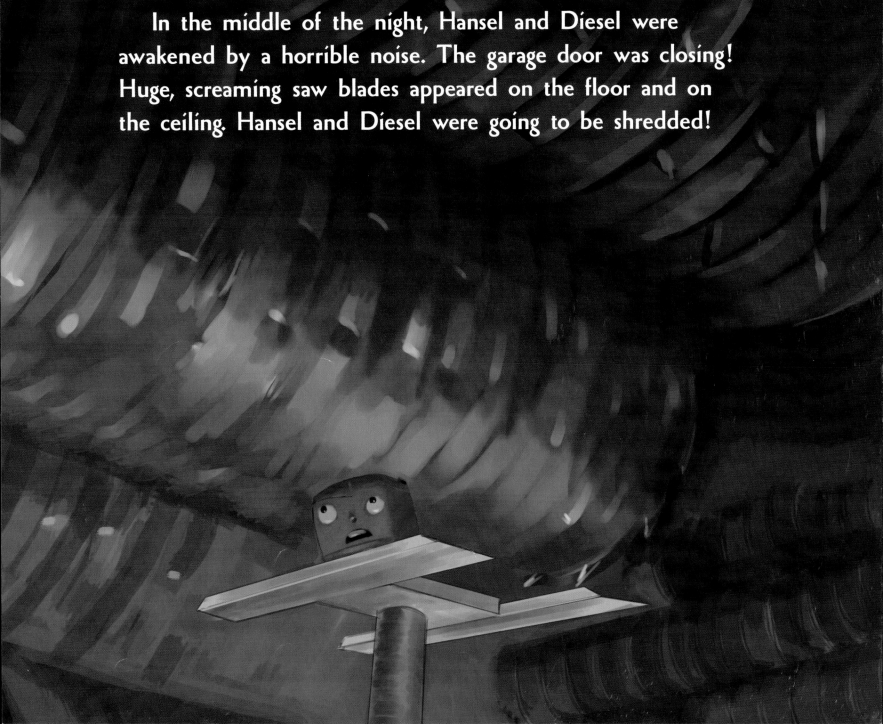

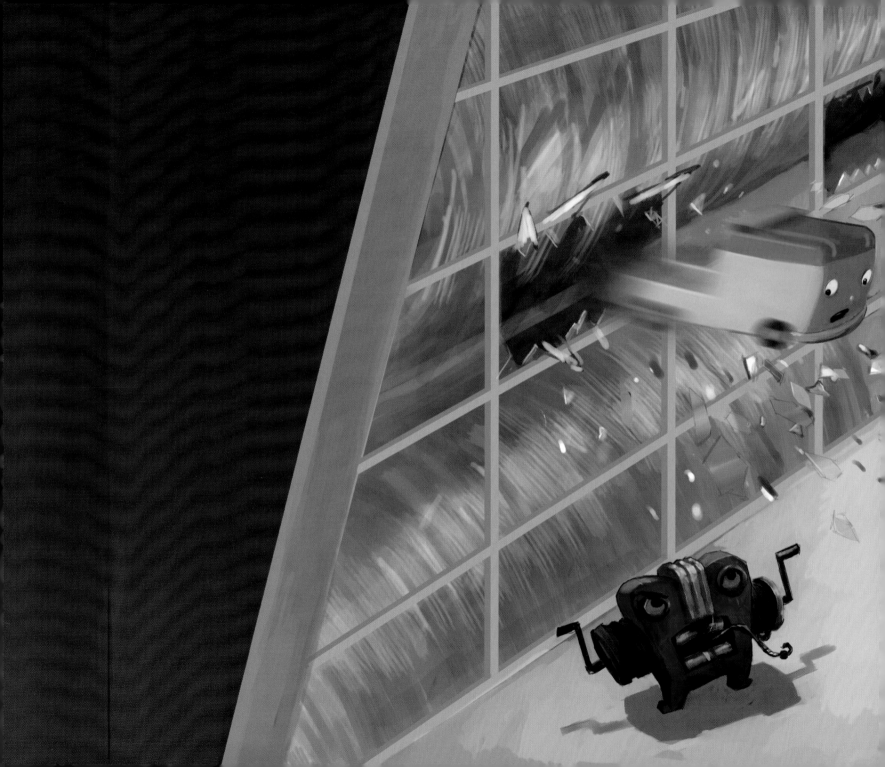

Diesel moved fast. Hansel moved even faster. They revved their engines and crashed through the glass of the garage door, flying over the winch, who was laughing out loud. "You Wicked Winch!" they yelled.

Hansel and Diesel raced into the mountains of junk. Although the snow had started to melt, they couldn't find the trail home.

"Don't worry, Diesel," said Hansel, trying to be brave. "At least we won't freeze. It's getting warmer."

As they stood there, trying to decide where to go, the end of a cable suddenly wrapped itself around Hansel and Diesel. Hansel and Diesel raced their engines and spun their wheels, but they couldn't escape the long reach of the Wicked Winch's cable!

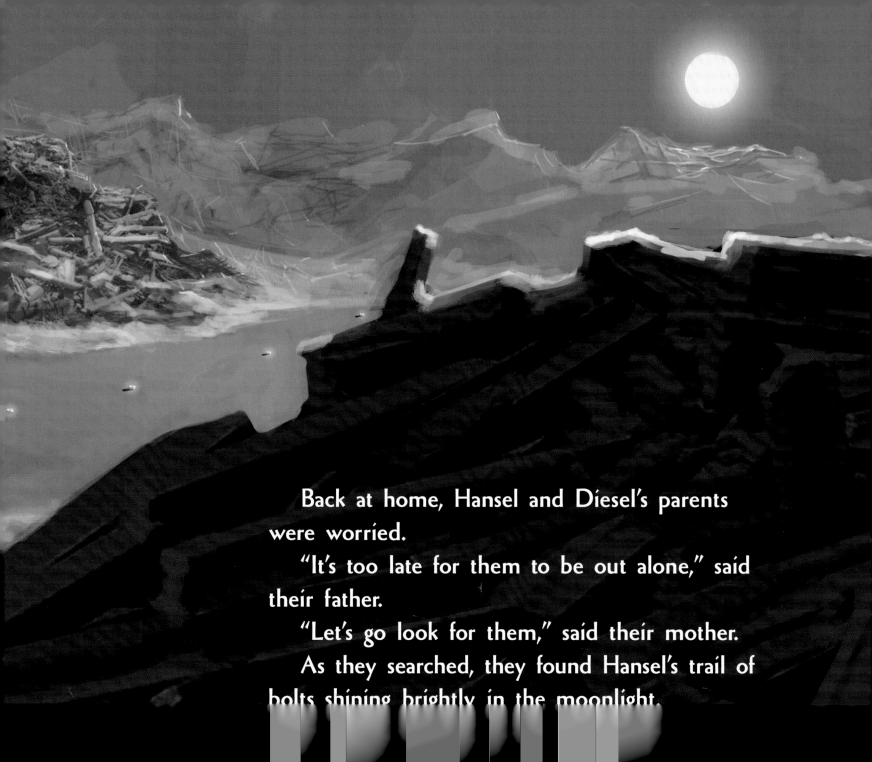

Back at home, Hansel and Diesel's parents were worried.

"It's too late for them to be out alone," said their father.

"Let's go look for them," said their mother.

As they searched, they found Hansel's trail of bolts shining brightly in the moonlight.

While Hansel and Diesel's parents were following the trail of bolts, they heard horrendous honks of terror. The children were being pulled into the Wicked Winch's shredder! Their father's powerful engine roared

Slowly he pushed her back into her garage of doom, where she was shredded into a thousand tiny scraps of metal.

"Yay!" cried Hansel and Diesel.

"Don't you ever leave home and scare us like that again!" said their father.

The family decided to move out of their old garage into the beautiful gas station, where they had plenty of fuel.